(Almost) Average Anthology

tales of adventure, loss, and oddity

Jason J. Nugent

DEDICATION

To my family, Sam Bell, and Aaron Hamilton.
Thanks for believing.

CONTENTS

INTRODUCTION

Most of the stories contained in this volume were published on my blog almostaverageblog.wordpress.com from October 2014 to November 2015 in slightly different forms. They've been edited and revised for this edition. There are also a couple unreleased stories exclusive to this collection.

These 16 stories cover a wide range of speculative fiction. There's horror, sci-fi, or fantasy elements in each story. It's an eclectic group but one I hope you'll find interesting and enjoyable.

I appreciate you taking a chance on these stories. I'm always open to feedback and would love to hear from you.

It means a lot to have you read my stories.

Thanks!
-Jason

jnugent@rocketmail.com
Twitter: @LailokenRi

STORY ONE
SEBASTIAN (I AM DEATH)

———————⊱———————

I am Death. I've always been, I will always be. Some have tried to stop me, but yet here I am. Ready to pounce, ready to strike, ready to take what I want. I have many names, but none suit me like Death. I. Am. Death.

I lurk unseen by everyone, yet I am always present. I see you though you do not fear me. I watch you carefully, calculating, but you don't notice it. I relish those times when you try to ignore me because that's when I strike. You can't deny me, you can't run far enough away from me. I will get you, I always get my prey. You may avoid me temporarily, but none escape my touch.

But I so enjoy being lazy. It makes you careless. You turn away from my terror. You lose sight of what I am. Nothing brings me greater satisfaction. You assume you're safe, but in an instant I strike. When I do, what can you do about it? Nothing. That control I have over you is intoxicating. I get drunk off my madness and I always want more. Lulling you into believing I am not here makes the end so much more gratifying. Please, please ignore me as I sit here being lazy.

Sometimes I enjoy playing with my prey. Watching you squirm and struggle in my grasp perks my ears up and my heart races. My eyes light up. Your frantic struggles make my mouth water. The tease, the back and forth, now that gets me going. Just as you feel safe, I crush you harder. I enjoy letting you think escape were possible. You get so excited. Your eyes betray the hope within. Hope motivates.

Hope forces a struggle. Your effort keeps me interested. So, I let you have your hope. I let you feel as though you are moments away from escape and then I strike harder. It's not fair to you, but what do I care? I am Death. This is what I do.

I see black and white. I don't see shades of gray or vibrant color as some say. I see only death and life. My job is to take life, and for that I need nothing other than black and white. Terror needs no color. My actions bring only black. Dark and light, black and white. You see light, you see color, you see hope. I perceive none of that. I see light that needs the dark. I see white that needs the black. Some say I recognize other than black and white, but they're wrong. They think they know me as though I'm an old friend. None know me like that.

I'm but a temporary companion. You want more of me because you are foolish. You don't fear what you can see, but what you see isn't real. Those who get to know me do so when I am there for a purpose. I don't "make friends." I bring death. You're lucky, you get to appreciate me because I allow it. But who says I'm not lulling you into complacency? I am Death after all.

I sit in the company of others for the briefest of times. I may appear to be listening like a good friend, but I'm not. I don't care about you. I don't care about anything other than death. I'll snuggle up to you, I'll stay close. That makes you happy. That gives you security. And you're a fool. I'm toying with you. You're my pet at that moment. I own you. And it's all just a game. I don't care about your past. My purpose is to take your future when I want. To deprive you of life when I deem it ready.

Do you understand yet? I'm not here for you. I'm here for myself and nothing else. Am I selfish? Do I carry narcissistic tendencies? Am I self-absorbed? Does it matter? You will never realize what I truly think. To you I'm something benign, something you can pass over. For your recklessness, I say thank you.

I lay here lazy and waiting. You mention something. The sounds come out as "See-Bass-Shun." I'm sure it's your way of saying "Death." You stroke my head unaware how close you are to losing your hand and maybe something worse. I begin my death sounds, the slow rumble within my throat, but you stroke my head more. Go on. My death sound transfixes you, to capture you, to trap you.

You expect I have a greater purpose. That's all part of the facade. Go on believing it. One day, it will catch up to you. But by then it will be too late. It's always too late for my prey. You will never know it's too late, but I will. Your time is mine to take. I am Death.

STORY TWO
THE BARN

⁓

The waning light of day held the barn in a wonderful silhouette against the orange and pink and purple sky. The sun peeked above the roofline of the gray weathered barn. It sat in the midst of a sea of golden-brown grain on a late winter day. In the distance were tractors and grain silos, quiet now with the harvest season over.

Mark approached the barn. He needed to gather seeds stored for his garden. He started the plants indoors so when spring pushed its way through winter's cold grasp, he'd be ready to transplant the seedlings outside and have his vegetables to the local market faster than anyone else in the county. Some had picked up on his techniques and were doing the same, but he started years ago and had the process down to an exact science.

He marveled at the vibrant colors splashed across the sky. The perfect blends of color in the air made it seem as though he stood face to face with a great masterwork of art. He smiled.

As he approached the barn door, he heard a soft rustle inside and hesitated. No one should be inside and the sound gave him pause. He waited, listening. The wind whistled through the tall dry grass. But nothing came from inside the barn. Laughing at his paranoia he pulled the door open.

He regretted it at once.

Staring back at him were bright yellow and green eyes. He couldn't tell how many creatures there were. Eyes were everywhere. He thought there were more than two per head. Maybe three or four but he couldn't be sure. All of those eyes, some bright yellow and some an eery green, stared at him as though he were the interloper and they belonged in the barn.

"He," one creature said. "He the one for seed," it continued in a broken english, somewhat like a child learning to speak.

"He," they said in unison. The chorus of voices overwhelmed Mark. Gray bodies moved and writhed, arms flailing as they approached him.

"He," they said again in one voice.

Mark's eyes widened. He lost the ability to scream. His focus remained on the mass of thin gray bodies with their luminescent eyes peering back at him.

"He," they said louder.

Mark tried to turn away but an unseen force held him like a statue. Panic grew inside of him threatening to overtake control of his mind.

One of the creatures stepped from the mass of gray and approached Mark. It was shorter than Mark and had three eyes. Two in the usual location and another on its forehead. Its eyes glowed bright green. Stopping a few feet in front of Mark, it held out a hand pointing a long skinny finger with a black fingernail at him.

"He…he makes seed. We need seed. We need get ready."

Mark felt his crotch go warm and damp. The scream inside still not voicing itself as though something held it in check. The gray creature took another step closer and placed his hand on Mark's forehead. Its cold touch was painful, but Mark couldn't shout or scream. The intense pain burrowed deep in his skull.

"He!" the mass behind the creature shouted. The creature closed its eyes and pulled back its hand, bringing Mark's brain with it. Mark's body fell to the ground, a massive hole in his forehead where it extruded his brain.

"He!" shouted the creatures. "He! He! He!"

The creature turned back to the mass of gray bodies, holding

Mark's bloody brain in his hands like an offering. They pushed themselves back, opening a pathway for the creature to walk. It stepped forward until it reached the center of the barn. Two of the strange creatures dug a hole with their black nailed hands in the hard dirt. The creature sniffed the brain, salivating, before placing it in the soil. The other two creatures that dug the hole covered Mark's brain with the soil.

"He!" those around them shouted. "He! Seed!"

They stood watching the ground, waiting for the seedling to grow.

***

The weathered gray barn stood in fields of grain, unimportant and unassuming. The winds blew harsh against it. Shades of blue with white wispy clouds colored the sky.

The seedling sprouted.

"He!" they shouted in unison. "Food," they said together.

STORY THREE
BENEATH THE CLOUDS

———⚭———

Jonah flew in his personal flight vehicle, or PFV, dodging buildings and traffic. The sunshade drawn down protected him from harmful flare-ups and reflections off the buildings. It was another flight home after a long day and week of work. He needed this weekend badly.

He engaged the auto-pilot hoping to relax on the three-hundred mile flight back home and drifted off to a fitful nap. It technically wasn't outlawed to nap while flying, but certainly frowned on. Jonah figured it wouldn't be long before a do-gooder with an axe to grind got the law passed. But for now he took his chances while the PFV flew a familiar course on its way back home.

Jonah finally fell deep asleep when his PFV made a sudden course correction that jolted him sideways smacking his head against the sturdy glass windshield. "Ouch! What are you doing you stupid thing?" he said. The reinforced glass didn't budge or crack when his head slammed against it. A knot started growing on his forehead.

His PFV didn't reply as it continued its flight. Jonah looked out at the buildings protruding through the clouds and grew alarmed. He wasn't sure if the hit on the head caused it or if it came from being somewhere he'd never seen before. The buildings looked different.

He was used to flat roof tops with green plants and trees or gardens and swimming pools. What he saw now were sharp tips of sleek buildings that extended much higher than he remembered any building going.

Frantic, he checked both sides of the PFV noticing several spire topped buildings on either side of him, glass and metal reflecting the evening sun. "Where am I?" he said. He clicked the onboard nav system. "Computer, where are we?"

"Cordero sector, section 19-563" the female nav voice explained. Jonah frowned. *Cordero* he thought. *Why are we here? And where is Cordero?* "Computer, return to home course at once," he said.

Nothing.

"Computer, return to home course now!" he said louder.

"Course set," the nav system replied. The PFV didn't change direction but continued towards the tallest of the spired buildings Jonah spotted far ahead.

He didn't notice it at first, but as he looked around, he saw that the traffic had dropped off to the point where it ceased completely.

Jonah switched the nav system to manual. He grabbed the steering wheel and tried turning but the PFV didn't change course. The switch didn't work. "What the…" Jonah said. A manual reboot of the system, a tricky maneuver while flying, was the next option. When he tried it nothing turned off. The entire PFV defied his attempts and continued its course toward the spired building growing larger in view as he approached.

Frustrated, Jonah stopped trying to reboot the PFV and decided to wait until it reached whatever destination it planned before he'd either have it repaired or grab public transport to take him home.

All day he dreamed of going home to relax and do nothing all weekend. This delay aggravated him. He didn't need this after the terrible week he had.

Without warning, the PFV dove and banked to the left, circling the large spire topped building until it set down on a landing pad on the opposite side of the building just above the clouds.

The PFV powered down and opened its hatch, the ladder extending to the platform. Jonah looked around and saw no one. Hesitating a moment, he climbed out of the defective PFV. "Why not, it's better to be out of that stupid machine than in it I guess," he said as he climbed down.

He'd rather be home sipping a cold beer and watching mindless television but instead found himself in "Cordero Sector" and he was lost. There was a door at the end of the landing pad that he assumed led to someone who might be able to help.

When he stepped inside he found himself in a corridor with sleek black walls. Fluorescent blue lights illuminated the halls to either direction, but no desk and no sign of help. Jonah spotted an elevator to his right. He walked over and smashed the only button available. Within moments a whoosh indicated the hyper-speed elevator approached his floor. The doors opened with a chime and he stepped inside. There were only four buttons on the control panel.

"What the hell?" he said. From the looks of the building on the outside, there must have been at least a hundred floors, yet there were only four buttons with one word on each. The top button was labeled "Food." The next button was labeled "Restroom." The third button was labeled "Sleep," while the bottom button was labeled "Home." Jonah hesitated, unsure what button to press. "Well," he said, then pressed the bottom button.

At once the elevator rushed downwards. Jonah steadied himself on the wall as g-forces pulled on him. The trip lasted well over a minute. Even in a hyper-speed elevator, that was a long time. And that worried him.

No one had been to "street level" in his lifetime, at least not that he knew. Ever since the Winter Wars raged across the planet, the surface of Earth had been nothing but a heaving mass of pollution. The surface boiled from nuclear waste and the evaporation rose up to create the man-made clouds that blocked the sun from ever reaching it. Above them, the world looked beautiful and inviting, but from the pictures he saw in history books and the news, the surface below was uninhabitable. It was utter waste and destruction.

Jonah considered the war and environment as the elevator slowed until it finally stopped, opening with a chime. Outside the elevator was a sleek black corridor very much like the one he left moments earlier. He hesitated but stepped out hoping to find anyone to help him. The elevator doors closed and the whoosh sound indicated its ascent.

Jonah turned right and walked along the hallway until he came to a door on his left. The corridor was silent. With a shaky hand he grabbed the handle and pushed. To his surprise, it opened.

Going through the door was like entering a different world. He stood in a large enclosure that was like nothing he'd ever seen. Glass walls stretched upwards curving above him. Outside he could see lush vegetation. Snow covered mountains rose high in the distance and birds danced in the air. It looked light outside as though the sun shone down here, but that was impossible. Everyone knew it couldn't penetrate the dense clouds. He looked on the verdant world before him with wonder and astonishment. He'd never seen anything so beautiful in his life. The problems of his week felt petty and worthless compared to the awesome beauty he gazed on.

Jonah walked along the glass lined enclosure enthralled by the trees and colorful flowers on all sides. At the end of the corridor was another door made of glass. Above it in bright green letters it read "HOME." He smiled and tried the handle. It opened.

A rush of warm tropical air washed over Jonah as he opened the door. Unfamiliar yet utterly pleasing scents mesmerized him. The sound of rushing water and birds chirping filled his ears. "Home," he said in bewilderment.

Stepping into the warm air, the lush beauty overwhelmed Jonah. All he knew were clouds and skies, nothing like the verdant landscape in front of him.

Home he thought over and over again. Suddenly his thoughts turned to his real home, to his PFV, to the towers above the skies and he worried he might be intruding on something malevolent. But the green expanse in front of him and the water rushing and the animals making sounds comforted him.

"Where am I?" he said.

"Why, you're home Mr. Pelinski," a familiar female voice said.

Jonah jumped to the side, his heart racing fast. He hadn't seen anyone when he entered the tropical garden.

"Who…who are you?" he said through shallow breaths. His heart thumped faster.

"Please do not worry Mr. Pelinski. You are safe, you are home," said a small robot, about the size of a cat. It sounded exactly like his PFV. Jonah hadn't seen it sitting motionless when he entered through the door. It blended with the surrounding rocks. The wondrous colors captivated him and he didn't notice anything else.

Jonah looked at the small robot with trepidation. It looked like a mini-human with two legs, two arms, and a face with eyes, nose, and a mouth though Jonah couldn't understand why.

"You are home Mr. Pelinksi. It was your time. We have brought you here because you belong. This is for you Mr. Pelinksi. You can roam free here," the tiny robot said in that familiar voice with a theatric wave of its arm. The robot was entirely gray except for its yellow glowing eyes.

"But, I don't understand," Jonah replied rubbing his head considering the robot's words.

"Understanding is not required Mr. Pelinksi. Just accept. It is yours. There are others, but you are all welcome. You are home," the robot repeated.

Jonah stared above the small robot's head in the distance.

Others? It was my time? he thought.

Jonah's eyes grew large as he remembered the jolt in his PFV and his head crashing against the window.

"Where am I?" he said again to the robot. It looked up at Jonah and a smile formed on its metallic face.

"You are home Mr. Pelinksi. This is Paradise, what you call the afterlife."

STORY FOUR
AIMEE'S QUEST

———————⌒———————

I stood on the cliff's edge with my long brown hair blowing in the wind, shielding my eyes against the sun as I stared at the dark forbidding castle below. I've travelled many days in search of Castle Morrigan, and there it stood in its gory beauty. I knew going there might mean I never return. It was the price I intended to pay. I had no choice.

Borma the dark wizard kidnapped my beloved Aimee and brought her to this decrepit castle. I followed the trail, alone but for my unfailing partner Brida. Brida is a snowcat, immense in size with a temper just as large. She protects me fiercely. I've had her since she was a cub and now full grown, she inspires fear in others and safety in me. Without Brida, I might never have made it.

And there we stood, the wind tussling her white fur this way and that while I looked at that castle of misery.

"Brida, we've made it," I said. She turned her head at me then towards the castle, growling as though she knew what lay ahead.

We followed a well-worn path that ran down the cliff crossing back and forth until we reached the bottom. I knew any guards could spot us, but at this point I didn't care anymore.

In my head I envisioned Aimee chained in a dungeon, dark and afraid. It fueled my anger. More than once I used that anger to push myself harder and farther in search of her. Looking on the place of her captivity, it blinded me with rage. Nothing would stop me now. Not even a herd of snowcats or a kith of giants. My anger burned ever brighter.

I unsheathed my sword and approached the castle, its dark gloomy walls rising higher in the air. In a masterful show of power, the castle builders settled the castle in such a way as to force visitors into a shallow valley making the castle seem taller. This effect gave intruders the illusion of immense power and magnificence as they looked on the now taller castle walls. I felt its weight hovering over me but I couldn't let it overcome my singular focus on recovering Aimee.

The castle itself was in ruins, hardly ever used anymore. It was far from the cities and its significance faded.

It was perfect for Borma, the dark wizard of the mountain. Once forced from his refuge in the snow capped Middle Mountains, he retreated to this desolate dwelling, knowing none would stop him. I believed he'd have guards serving him and approached as though he did, wary of a crossbow bolt yet still carried forward by my anger and rage.

The gate was open. I heard nothing from inside. Brida growled a low menacing sound, the kind that often forced her prey to flee in terror. We walked inside and found ourselves in a large courtyard. It was gray and dirty, the walls rising around us. I noticed many of the crenellations were crumbling or missing altogether.

It was so quiet leading me to think maybe the occupants fled. I feared Aimee might no longer be held captive within those drab decaying walls.

The only place we could go was up a flight of stone steps to our right. The top of the steps opened to a landing with a large arched wooden door.

We approached wary of an impending ambush. Brida crept at my side, the hair on the back of her neck bristling. As we neared the door, I jumped and held my sword in front of me as a raven that must have roosted in a broken section of the wall near the door burst out, flapping its black wings and cawing at us madly. My heart beat faster and faster until I calmed myself when I realized what happened. Brida's eyes were wild. "It's fine Brida, just a filthy raven," I said calming her.

I stepped to the door anticipating the worst. I knelt closer listening for sounds on the other side, but it was quiet. Suspicious of hidden surprises inside the door, I crashed through it, hoping to catch any guard inside unaware. I tumbled forward into darkness, falling to the floor. Brida followed me inside, growling and scanning the room.

It was empty and silent.

I stood up confused, dusting myself. I had to be in the right place. "Brida girl, where are they?" I asked. She sniffed around and ran down a dark hallway. "Brida, wait!" I called out.

I spotted a torch on the wall. Sheathing my sword and reaching into the bag around my waist, I took out flint and steel igniting the tar soaked torch. It took a bit of time but lit, flooding the room with its warm light. With the torch in one hand, I drew my sword as I followed the dark corridor in search of Brida.

I tracked her paw prints in the thick layer of dust on the stone floors until I came to a large room that had a small bed of dirty rushes and a desk with a chair. Brida stood in front of the desk sniffing and growling. "What is it girl, do you smell something?" She didn't turn her head. On the desk lay a piece of parchment. I approached curious. Laying my sword on the desk I picked up the parchment, reading it by the torchlight.

You are persistent Finn. However I am much too clever to let you catch me here. Your darling Aimee is alive but no longer here. When you read this, she will be with me in another castle. Her blood is important. I need her pure crimson blood for my greatest spells. Fear not, I will not let her die. I wish you could understand, but alas I know you do not.

-B

"No!" I cried, my arms raised high. "Aimee where are you?" I bemoaned. Brida howled a hideous, terrifying sound.

My beloved was captive in another castle.

Red filled my vision. I vowed to search until I found her and killed that wretched Borma.

My search endures to this day.

STORY FIVE
VACATION

———————— ✦ ————————

Jim stood at the top of wooden stairs admiring the clear blue sea. The sight was magnificent. The stairs led down a rocky incline ending on the white beach below. He stood maybe fifty feet above the sea. Inhaling the warm ocean air, he closed his eyes and let the sun soothe him.

***

Recently his wife Meagan insisted they go to the sea. Insisted may have been too kind a word for Jim. She threw a tantrum demanding he take her to an island resort or else. They had a huge fight over it. Jim had no desire to go on vacation and he hated the beach. This was the busiest time of year at work. The last thing he needed was to leave on vacation. But, after Meagan badgered him for weeks, he gave in and asked off. He grumbled about it to her yet she didn't listen to a word he said. Her mind was on the beach, the sun, and drinks.

Before he knew it, Jim was paying for a trip to the Bahamas at a four-star all-inclusive resort. He hated to fly. He'd rather drive across the country for days instead of fly. Meagan knew it, but she set her heart on the Caribbean and the Bahamas called her like a long lost love.

"Jim," she said as they booked their trip, "this is wonderful! I'm so glad we took this vacation. I love the beach! I love the ocean. I can't wait to get there." Jim grunted. He thought about the sales he'd miss and the commission he'd lose because Meagan wanted to sun herself. She was oblivious to his concerns. Her smile annoyed Jim.

***

Jim stood at the stairs grinning. Meagan was right. This was a great idea. He let the stress of his job float away on the tropical breeze.

Jim lifted his heavy suitcase and walked down the weathered stairs, careful to balance himself against its weight. He reached the first landing and rested. Jim leaned against the wooden rail and watched a sailboat in the distance. The azure waters spread out before him like a welcoming blanket, ready to comfort and warm him. In the water he noticed a large dark gray manta ray swim by. The clear water allowed him to see every detail on the ray's back. He laughed to himself thinking how wrong he was for doubting Meagan.

An employee of the resort walked up the stairs and approached Jim.

"Can I help you with the bag sir?" he asked. He was dark-skinned and wearing a white linen shirt and matching shorts. He was cheerful and his name badge said "Jengo." Jim smiled.

"No thanks, I've got this. Just appreciating the view. It's wonderful out here." Jengo looked to the ocean and nodded.

"Yeah, it is heaven on Earth. Well, if you need anything, please ask. We're here to make your stay as pleasant as possible." He shook Jim's hand and walked back towards the resort.

Jim watched Jengo return to the resort and sighed. He should've done this a long time ago. The sales would still be there. He had an assistant that watched over his accounts while he was out and he did a great job of handling customers. The commission would still be there. *So what took you so long?* he thought to himself. Shaking his head, he picked up the heavy suitcase and walked down the last flight of steps, each board creaking under his weight.

When he reached the bottom, glorious white sand greeted him.

He removed his shoes, stuffed them in a side pocket of the suitcase, and let the warm sensation of the sand envelop his toes. He wiggled them in the sand, covering his feet. Smiling at himself more for not doing this sooner than anything else.

The resort was to his left but the beach extended far to his right where it curved to a point. It looked inviting and relaxing, so he picked up his heavy suitcase and trudged along the beach. Check-in could wait.

The rhythmic sounds of crashing waves soothed him as he walked on the beach. He found a quiet spot near the tip of the beach where he sat down on the sand, breathing heavy from carrying the suitcase. The closest person to him was climbing the stairs from the beach.

"I love it here!" he said to the waves. They replied, crashing on the sand in front of him.

Jim leaned towards his suitcase and unzipped the main compartment. His face beamed as he reached in the black bag. With a soft, delicate touch, he lifted out Meagan's head. He sat it on the sand, leaning it against the suitcase facing the ocean.

"We did it Meagan," he said, "we're on vacation!

STORY SIX
SPINE OF THE WORLD

———————— ✺ ————————

"They are beautiful, aren't they?" Lailoken asked. He and his snowcat Seraph sat along a high ridge overlooking a verdant valley dotted with brown and red. The late autumn air swirled around them. Seraph looked up, nudged her head against Lailoken's thigh and laid her head back down.

"The Spine of the Gods. Don't you know what this means?" he asked. Seraph didn't move. "Well, if you were any kind of snowcat you'd know. We're almost at the edge. Once we cross over, who knows what awaits us."

Lailoken gazed across the valley to where it ended in sheer gray cliffs rising high in the sky. They looked like a giant beast lay down and died, leaving an enormous skeleton. The cliffs rose like vertebrae in the sky from which it earned its name Spine of the Gods. From this vantage point, they looked impassable. What lay beyond - that was stuff of legends, where Lailoken and Seraph dared to go.

Lailoken rubbed Seraph's snowy white head. The giant cat purred a deep rattling sound. "Come on, we need to get there by nightfall," Lailoken said. The cat purred louder. "Seraph, come on now," Lailoken said as he stood, brushing the dirt and grass from his woolen pants. Seraph rose and stretched her long frame, letting her sharp nails poke from her paws as she did.

They took close to four hours making their way to the valley floor. They walked along a stream that bubbled and gurgled until they came to a small village nestled in the middle of the valley. There were two roads that intersected in the center of the village.

"Seraph, stay here until I can find a place to stay. They might not be too welcoming to a large snowcat like you," he said as he scratched her under her chin. She rubbed on his thigh almost knocking him over. "Seraph, you'll be safe out here. I'll be back soon." Lailoken walked towards the inn.

"Welcome to the Dark Dog Inn," the innkeeper said as Lailoken stepped inside. The room was dusty but comfortable. Once inside, Lailoken froze. The innkeeper's head was that of a giant dog, like a retriever. He'd never seen a real caninian and the sight of one startled him.

"A stranger, eh?" the dog faced innkeeper asked. His face was deep brown with large brown eyes and a full set of teeth. His long ears hung to his shoulders.

Lailoken struggled for words.

"Yeah, you aren't from around here. Not too many visitors from out of the valley." The innkeeper raised his snout and sniffed the air. "You brought a snowcat here?"

Lailoken looked at the innkeeper with a cocked eyebrow. "Yeah, yeah I did. She's harmless though. She won't bother anyone. I was looking for a place we could stay. But…"

"But what? We can't handle a snowcat around here?" The innkeeper snorted. "We're caninian, but we are civilized. My name's Gorthe. Welcome," he said and flashed a smile that was at once warm and threatening. He reached out a hand that was all human. Lailoken hesitated then shook it.

"Come, let's get you settled. So what brings you here?" Gorthe asked. He motioned for Lailoken to follow him down a hall to a small room at the end.

"Just passing through," Lailoken said. Gorthe eyed him and nodded.

"Here you are," he said waving a hand to the empty room. "You can stay here, but your snowcat will have to stay outside in the stables. No animals are allowed in the inn," Gorthe said. Lailoken wanted to protest, to say how could half-dogs say any such thing, but thought better of it.

"Thank you Gorthe. I must show Seraph where she can stay." Lailoken walked back to where he left Seraph. He found her laying in the tall grass away from the road watching for people.

"You won't believe it Seraph. They're caninians!" Seraph didn't flinch. "Did you hear me girl? They are half-dogs! I thought those were just myths." Seraph licked her paws. "Well come on, I found us a place to stay." Seraph rose and trotted to Lailoken's side. She followed him on the road to the inn where he led her to the stables.

"It's not the best, but it'll do. I'll bring food later. Rest up, tomorrow we go to the Spine."

The night passed without incident. Gorthe gave them a few small loaves of dense bread for the trip and wished them well. Lailoken and Seraph left before the little village woke from the cool night.

It took most of the day before they were at the base of the Spine. The steep cliffs rose high into the clouds where they couldn't see the top. Seraph growled as they stood marveling at the sight. "What is it girl? This has been our destination. We're going through and crossing to the other side." The snowcat licked her paws unconcerned.

Lailoken pulled a map from out of his sack, unrolled it and pondered. He scoured over the ancient markings. "Ahh, yes there it is," he said then rolled it up and put the map away. "Seraph, we go this way," he said pointing to a deep crack in the solid wall. As they approached the crack Seraph's ears perked up at the sound of a low humming noise.

They walked closer and stopped just outside the crack. Inside Lailoken watched in wonder as a glowing portal in hues of blue and purple shimmered before him. The hair on Seraph's back stood up. She growled a deep menacing threat. "Seraph," he said, stroking her massive head, "it's ok. This is the way through the Spine. We step in there and we find our destination on the other side. It's everything we've wanted." She hesitated as Lailoken stepped forward. "Come on, let's go," he called to her. With a hesitation uncommon to her, Seraph walked towards him.

Lailoken stepped in the shimmering portal first, his leg breaking the vertical plane. Seraph followed. Just as her head broke through the portal, Lailoken heard a shout behind him.

"No! Stop! Don't go in there!" Gorthe came running towards them, his large ears flapping with each step. Lailoken looked back at him confused. "Stop! The caninians did this once! Don't go in there!"

It was too late. Lailoken's momentum carried him forward. When he stepped through the portal, a new race of beings emerged on the other side. They came to be known as the felinians.

STORY SEVEN
THE END

I stood looking out over the vast expanse of desert before me. The sun baked sand stretched as far as my eyes could see. Dunes rose and sank in a haphazard pattern. I found this oasis to shield me from the brutal sun. I leaned against a palm tree wondering what to do next. The prospect of going back out into the desert didn't appeal in the slightest. As far as I was concerned, I'd stay here forever. I had shade, there were a few plants, and I saw an insect or two. Surely I could live off of that.

My inner man, the one that often kicked me into gear, told me to forget it. He was right. I act like I can't hear him. Who wants to always acknowledge they're wrong to someone else? But when it came down to it, he only had my best interests at heart. Damn him!

I turned from the brown sea of sand ahead of me and sat at the base of the tree. I had a backpack full of basics: a cup, matches, a small rope, extra clothes, and a bible. I carried a large bowie knife that stayed on me at all times. I learned the hard way never to let it out of my sight. The heavy canvas olive-drab military backpack held all I possessed in this world. I was lucky. Most everyone else these days have far less.

It must have been several months, maybe a year back everything went to hell. I honestly can't say when. I lost my watch, my cell phone died a few full moons ago and I have no idea how many days have passed. I stopped counting the sunrise and sunsets some time back. And it's not like there's internet access anywhere near here. I suspect it might not be available anywhere. Not anymore. I guess its for the best since that's how everything started.

Hunger follows me everywhere I go. I thought I was closer to civilization now, but by the looks of it, I'm far from it. I haven't had a decent meal in weeks. I've lived off bugs and assorted vegetation. As long as it's not rotten, I've eaten it. I've had to. My once svelte thirty-four inch waist is now much smaller. If I had to guess, I'd say I'm down to Beiber size. Things are way out of hand. We were never supposed to get this way.

I need water in a bad way. I've started hallucinating. I think I see zombies wandering the desert or other times I've seen Washington crossing the Delaware, but the river is sand and Washington is Hulk Hogan. I've seen bizarre things out here. If I do make it back to the real world, I hope my mind joins me.

I looked around and watched the green plants fade away. The tree I leaned on winked out of existence and I fell to the hot sand. Another hallucination. I need to get out of here quick. If I stay much longer in this wasteland, I'll end up a part of it and no one will know the truth. I need to get moving. The sun was not yet overhead, which meant I had time to walk before the real heat kicked in. Once it reaches its peak, there's nothing to do but hide under my backpack and ride it out. That's a way better choice versus spending my energy fighting the brutal sun.

My inner man always has energy and he uses it to get me up and going. One day I'd like to either beat him to a pulp or shake his hand. Maybe both.

I stood on shaky legs, slung my backpack over my shoulder, and walked. I had no specific destination. I went east. Why? I can't say. I figured I'd rather have the sun at my back if I needed to walk in the late afternoon. It's as simple as that. As much as the world went haywire, I knew that the sun still rose in the east and set in the west, so with that logic, I followed the rising sun, allowing it to get behind me as I traveled east.

As a way of getting my mind off the numbing blindness of the desert ahead, I ran through the events of the last days in my head looking for the moment it spiraled out of control and forced me to this blasted desert. I focused most of the blame on the "program."

The world got to a point where we were connected with everything. Phones, computers, cars, watches, and things as innocuous as toys and groceries, all these were controlled and manipulated through our interconnectedness. You could say the internet became like veins and arteries, giving and taking blood to us, the people, and taking it back to the heart, which wasn't a real heart but a network of supercomputers that regulated everything. All commerce tied back to this array of computers. All financial, social, and medical systems did as well.

We didn't know this. All we knew was life was getting "better" with every new version of our gadgets. We eagerly plopped down money to finance our own enslavement.

I belonged to a loose knit underground organization bent on exposing this network. We understood the engineering behind it and we worked tirelessly together, though anonymously, to find a way into its infrastructure to tell the world about it. Our goals were noble. We didn't want to hurt anyone, just free us from this blindness, from the slavery we had unwittingly put ourselves into. We didn't understand we could topple governments, or crash stock markets, or incite international war. All we specialized in were computer programs. We knew enough about this network to introduce a small trojan horse virus to the system intending to track it to its source.

One of our guys, he went by the name "Snoopy," let loose a program intended to piggyback along the communications pathways of the main supercomputers to find their location and share that with the world. Our main goal was to expose how much we've allowed computers to rule our world, not to harm the system but to enlighten people on the inherent dangers of putting our fate at the mercy of machines only able to process the living world in 0's and 1's.

That simple program had a bug in it that caused a catastrophic failure of the entire network system. Governments couldn't function, banks shut down, people panicked, weapons systems went on the fritz. The world went crazy.

It's funny when you look back at it. All those so-called "Third-World" countries held out longer than the rest. Since they didn't have the infrastructure to be "modernized" like most of the world, they suffered the least amount of upheaval. That changed when the "modern" nations went to war and the smaller nations became collateral damage inside the carnage. All because of a mistake in computer code.

I don't know Snoopy and I don't know where he's at, or if he's still alive. Before the end, he lived in Singapore. I don't know if Singapore is even there anymore. I guess it doesn't matter.

I need to keep moving to the east. Eventually I'll find my way out of here. The sun is getting hotter and higher overhead telling me I need to rest. I need to save what energy I have left.

I must continue because someone needs to know. We didn't mean it. It was nothing more than a glitch in computer code.

Until then, I'll be laying here under my backpack for a while.

STORY EIGHT
THE SEA

The soft glow of the day's fading light warmed Kathryn. She used to go on these beach walks with her husband all the time. Doing so now with her son, the pain still felt so fresh. Her husband used to tease her that walking along the beach stirred feelings inside him that needed release. She always assumed something sexual, but it turned out she had the wrong assumption.

"Mom, look at this," her ten year old son James said. He still carried a sense of wonderment to him at his age. He'd started fifth grade earlier in the year and as much as he pretended to be a big boy, he still showed glimpses of her little boy. She treasured those moments, knowing they were fleeting and soon he'd be grown and want nothing to do with her. "Check this out mom," he said holding up his hands to her. She looked and jumped. "James! What is that?" she asked. She feared spiders and crickets and other creepy things and this little creature looked odd to her. "I'm not sure. I think it's a crab or something. Can I keep it?" He looked up at her with soft blue eyes and she almost fell for it. "No leave it here. I won't have something creepy like that in my house." He frowned and let the creature go. It scurried along the white sand and went in a hole.

The two of them walked in silence listening to the distant birds and the soft waves on the beach. The calm ocean fit Kathryn's mood perfectly. She could stand there all night thinking and observing. She didn't need constant stimulation from a television or a computer. Give her the beach and solitude and she'd be in heaven.

It was James who broke the silence.

"So mom, what are we gonna do?" She stopped walking and looked at him. He looked so much like his father it hurt. "What?" he asked. "What are we gonna do? I'm serious. I can handle it mom." She shook her head but didn't reply. Instead, she walked out to the water till it covered her ankles.

The ocean felt warm. Warmer than she expected for this time of year. Winter would be on its way soon, but for now, the warm breeze coming in off the water took those thoughts away, gently blowing her long curly hair behind her. She waded in the tranquil water watching as tiny fish swam around her ankles. She stepped carefully in the soft sand not wanting to step on a busted shell. James walked alongside her. "Mom," he began again, "what are we gonna do? We need to do something." She hoped to avoid this with James and enjoy the serenity of the beach, but he had other plans.

"I'm not sure James," she began at last. "I refuse to think about it for now. Couldn't we enjoy the water and the breeze?"

He looked at her with his mouth open ready to say something, then closed it as she turned away. "Whatever mom," he mumbled. She tried shrugging off his attitude, not wanting it to shake her moment. She breathed in the salty air, letting it fill her with hope and promise.

Finally she talked.

"James, listen, I know you want to know what our next move is, but you must be patient. I understand that's hard for you, but please, let me work it out."

"But mom," he started before she held up her hand to stop him. His face turned red as he stopped talking. Silently she thanked him and walked along the beach, her feet splashing in the warm water.

When they reached the parking lot where they left the car, Kathryn stopped James. "OK, listen. I will say this once. Got it?" James nodded his head. "Good. Your father," she began, "he was a bad man. I don't like talking ill of him because without him, you

wouldn't be here. But the truth is," she paused unsure if she should continue. "Come on mom, it's ok," James urged. She noticed they were alone in the parking lot.

"Your father, he did many bad things. He," she paused, trying to find the right words, "he got caught up in a fantasy. He wanted to live a pirate's life or something like that. He went to New Orleans to 'find a crew' as he said, and when he came back, he wasn't the same person." James looked up at Kathryn, his face showing confusion. "It sounds strange, but that's what happened. Remember his sailboat?" James nodded. "He didn't have that until you were five. He'd spend his summers going on long trips with his 'crew' and when he came back, he never would tell me what he did or where he went."

"I remember him being gone mom, but that didn't make him a bad man. He loved the sea and enjoyed sailing. He took me out a lot," James said. Kathryn closed her eyes. Telling her son the truth hurt.

"Son, your father had good in him, but he gave in to his dark side and those summer trips turned out to be nothing short of real piracy. Your father *was* a pirate. He and his crew went on a reign of terror. I tried to shield you from it as best I could. I told you he died from a heart attack, but it was much worse." She shifted feet, trying to steady herself. "He was murdered by someone he tried to rob. A drug lord from Mexico. So you ask about our next move? Our next move is to leave him in the past and go forward with our new lives ahead of us."

The boy's eyes went wide. "What do you mean 'reign of terror?'" he asked. He'd never heard that used about his father. Kathryn thought she misplaced her trust in James's capacity to understand the gravity of the situation. She spoke too much too soon to James. He was only ten.

"What I mean to say is that your father had problems. He's no longer a threat to our safety. We have each other and we are safe." James looked as though he bore holes right through her skull. The boy had a stare that discomforted her.

His gaze lost its strength when he looked over her shoulder out to sea. His eyes softened and he peered right past her. "Look!" he shouted as he pointed to the water. She turned to see a faint ship shimmering across the water. The tall sail had the numbers 569887 going down vertically. The entire ship wove in and out of view though it was only fifty yards from the shoreline. It was as though made of fog or mist. Kathryn's body shivered. She knew those numbers.

"No! You can't have him!" she shouted. She clutched James in her arms.

The boy paid no attention to her. His gaze fixed on the ship moving from east to west. He felt called to it as a bug to a light. He started walking in the sand towards the water. Frantic, Kathryn tried holding him back. "No!" she cried, "you must leave him! He's not for you. You cannot take him. James, please, snap out of it!" She shook the boy but he didn't react. He looked wistfully out to sea at the ship.

"Dad," he whispered.

Kathryn stood in front of James blocking his path. "No James, you cannot go out there! You must turn away, now! Please son, don't do this." Large tears streaked her face as she tried in vain to stop his march toward the sea. For a ten year old, he had enough strength to push her away and he knocked her to the sand. She tried scrambling up but it was too late. James waded out to the sea and headed straight for the ship. A figure stood on the deck waving as if to say hello, but she knew better. She ran to the water to stop James. Water splashed as she ran and the soft sand underneath held her back. She couldn't reach him in time.

James's head went slowly underwater. Bubbles gurgled up but soon stopped. "No!" she cried, "No damn you! That's my son!" She sobbed uncontrollably. As she stared at the winking ship, she recognized another, smaller figure appear standing next to her husband. She screamed and cried as the ship turned out to sea and drifted away.

STORY NINE
SOCIAL SECURITY

The knuckles on Gene's fat fingers turned white as he gripped the steering wheel. Perspiration beaded on his forehead in the mid morning sun. His head pivoted back and forth, scanning the street for trouble. He looked up at the light ahead, wishing and hoping for it to turn green. To the right he caught sight of her. She was about eighty years old and walking with a cane. Gene didn't think she looked in bad shape. His intel proved correct as the intersection of Lorain and West 130th, the intersection he now waited at, is where he spotted her right at the exact minute she should be there. The light turned green. With the back of his chubby hand he wiped his forehead. It was go time.

***

Despite all the alcohol abuse in his past and the spotty memories it created, Gene could pinpoint exactly the moment he got involved in his current profession, if one could call it that. He had gone to his weekly AA meeting at Annunciation Catholic Church on the west side of Cleveland. It was mid-winter and all the talk centered on the terrible weather and the burgeoning cost of healthcare because of recent legislation. To be honest, Gene didn't give a damn about government policies. The weather, sure, but all the rest didn't matter. However, staying sober concerned him.

He'd been an alcoholic for years, vodka his weakness. The cheap availability of the stuff allowed him to sink deeper and deeper into a life consumed by alcohol. He tried his best to drink his life away. His mom of all people convinced him he needed help. At first he grumbled and went to his initial meeting just to shut her up. Fortunately for him, he met a hot redhead there and came back the next week just to see her. It wasn't the most noble of intentions, but it got him there. In time he took the meetings seriously and got sober. By the time he went to that fateful mid-winter meeting, he'd been clean for about eight months.

At that meeting a sharp dressed man in his thirties gathered with them for the first time. The man wore a black fitted suit and had short brown hair. He reminded Gene of the movie Men in Black. Gene thought maybe an alien would jump out of nowhere and the man in the suit would shoot it with a cosmic death ray. His mind slipped off on tangents like that, more now he was sober. No alien emerged and no cosmic death ray gun appeared, but the man changed Gene's life almost as much as if he did.

When the meeting finished and they stood around outside smoking, the man approached Gene.

"So…vodka huh?" the man asked. Gene remembered him introducing himself as Allen, and he worked for the government, but he never said in what capacity.

"Yeah, it's been my nemesis for a long time. And…" Gene thought for a moment, trying to remember what Allen said in the meeting. "Whisky and mouthwash, right?" he said with his thick fingers lifted to his chin as though in deep thought. Reflexively he rubbed his beard.

Allen looked to the ground. "Yeah, that's it," he said. He looked up at Gene. The dark, cold night made Allen look menacing to Gene. He didn't know why. A strong urge to drink, something he hadn't had in a long time, grew inside him like a cancer.

"Say, what do you do for a living Gene? I don't remember what you said in there," Allen asked.

Gene shook his head. "That's cause I didn't. I'm unemployed at the moment. You could say I'm 'between' jobs right now. I've done a little bit of everything over the years though."

Allen smiled. "Do you know how to drive?"

Gene screwed up his face. "Well, yeah I do. Why?"

"I have an offer for you Gene. How'd you like a job with the government?"

That moment changed everything for Gene. He followed up with Allen and soon he began working for the US government. Officially he was part of Health and Human Services. His "official" position was as an inspector charged with making sure those he enrolled into Medicare and Medicaid due to recent legislation were not bilking the system. With the millions of expected enrollees, he had to make sure everything was legitimate. Millions of families across the country signed up meaning more money was required for those productive younger families.

Unofficially he had a much greater purpose. Under Allen's directive, his orders were to save the government money. Too many elderly people weren't contributing to the economic welfare of the nation burdening the system. And Allen promised a bonus for each one.

That's when Gene stopped going to his meetings.

***

Gene slammed his foot on the accelerator. The tires screeched, leaving a trail of smoke. The old lady with the cane had been about halfway across the road when she saw Gene's car. She dropped her cane, her arms shooting up. The last Gene remembered was her face twisted as if screaming. He smashed into her, her frail body thudding loudly on his car. She flew up in the air, tumbling over the roof and he watched in his rear-view mirror as her body crashed to the road, her legs and arms twisting in gruesome ways. He drove on, narrowly missing a bus crossing the road.

He reached to the floorboard and grabbed a bottle of vodka, its contents close to empty. He finished the last of it, tossing the bottle out the window, smashing into a thousand pieces on the street. Much like the old lady he just ran over.

"Another one off the books!" he yelled. He'd need to report to Allen soon to collect his bonus. His last one lay in tiny glass shards on the street behind him.

STORY TEN
SUNSHINE AND ASTEROIDS

A warm salty breeze blew in along palm trees sprouting from the water like cat tails. They formed two neat rows as though framing a wide boulevard, which they once had. The sun rose in the center of the water road as city planners envisioned many years ago. Though then, concrete lay between the palms, not the gently lapping water now occupying the space. The suns waking rays cast an alluring array of colors across the water. Tim stood and admired the morning beauty.

He woke on a small island where a gas station once stood. He remembered the out of state license plates that came there, paying for overpriced gas and soda on their way to the giant amusement parks farther south. He'd lived in Florida his entire life and resented those people with their smugness and disregard for natural beauty of the land. Now, they'd never visit again. And he was ok with that. At least he knew it once. He'd still be there when the receding waters revealed a new land, a new paradise, and he couldn't wait. If he lasted long enough.

Tim ran out of food long ago, forced to eat any bug or small water creature brave enough to land on his patch of land. He guessed he lost more weight than he used to think he needed to lose and the unrelenting sun baked his skin to a dark brown. He kinda liked that. He always found it hard to get tanned before. Now, once the waters went away, he'd be skinny and tanned, ready to be the man of some girl's dreams.

No one knew the asteroid was there until it was too late. Instead of crashing in the midst of a large metropolis, its trajectory took it to the center of the Atlantic. That was worse. Going out from all directions, a huge wave circled out and grew in size and intensity until it raced towards the shore lines of Africa, Portugal, and the east coast of Canada and the United States. The government tried to get the population moving west, but the majority of people thought they'd weather the storm like any other hurricane. That proved to be a mistake.

The waters rose several months ago, destroying everything in its path. At first, there was mass confusion. People didn't heed the tidal wave warning assuming they were too far inland to be affected. They were wrong. The enormous wave washed across the state, coming in from the Atlantic and crashing to the Gulf of Mexico. Tim discounted the radio and television warnings. His phone screamed at him as the state and then national weather services issued alerts.

Tim marveled at the rising sun and breathed in deep. Salty air filled his lungs. He exhaled loudly. "Yeah, that's the ticket," he said to no one. He stretched his arms high overhead, his tense muscles straining. His arms popped and creaked, making him think of his grandfather. His grandfather was such a vibrant, fun loving man. Tim pictured him sitting in a chair on the back patio, bloody mary in hand, smiling and joking. He missed his grandfather. Then he started reflecting on his situation.

As far as he knew, Tim was alone. He had seen no one in over two months. Airplanes, helicopters and the occasional boat sounded in the distance when it began. Tim yelled and jumped, flailing his arms to no effect. None of them ever stopped. Then after two weeks, they ceased and stayed silent. The only sounds now filling his ears were the rustles of palm branches and the gentle waves.

He tried to leave his island once, but when several alligators and a shark - a shark! followed him, Tim considered it safer on his small plot of dry land, so he set up camp and claimed it for his own. He spent the days yelling out for help or taunting the swiftly moving gators. Not once did the thought of them climbing up out of the water ever occur to him.

Tim watched the sun rise to its heights, the only show he had now, and sat still with his hands on his knees. The gnawing hunger in his stomach long ago turned to a constant feeling of emptiness he learned to ignore, mostly. Before long, Tim found he'd spent the entire day waiting, watching, and not moving. The sun set and darkness followed.

Black night covered the waters and stars filled the sky. If there was ever one thing Tim could be thankful for since the asteroid strike, it was the unending attraction of the night sky. He laid back on the cooling sand, mesmerized by the twinkling stars above. He made out the constellations: Orion, the Big Dipper, and many others he couldn't name. As he lay there, ready for another night of nocturnal beauty, something caught his eye.

Red streaked the sky. One after another bright red and orange streaks fell from above, like a hailstorm of fire. Tim furrowed his brow trying to understand. All around him, small red streaks smacked the water, huge cascading waves shooting up and out.

"What the…" Tim said as a rock the size of a quarter slammed into the sand just feet from him, forming a crater larger than twice the size of his head. Tim jumped and backed away from the crater, his arms shaking. He looked up again at the sky.

For a moment, he thought he saw the familiar red of his grandfathers bloody mary. It made him smile. The rock slammed his head, killing him instantly. He died with a smile, thinking about his grandfather.

STORY ELEVEN
JEB AND THE BARN

"Pa! Pa! Where ya at?" Jeb called. His dingy white shirt clung to his muscular frame underneath faded denim overalls. His greasy black hair slicked back from sweat barely covered the large scar that went from his left ear back to the base of his skull, Pa's reminder never to cross him. "Pa, damn it, where'd ya go?" he yelled, his hands cupping his mouth to amplify his voice.

Jeb walked down the porch steps to parched earth where grass once grew years ago kicking dust up with each step. His work boots so covered with the stuff it was hard to tell what color they used to be.

He stood, hands on his hips, scanning the yard for any sign of Pa. Other than an old Buick to his right with its hood propped open by a couple empty beer bottles, the only other things in the yard were several scrawny coon-hounds, their tails wagging as though it was feeding time. "Git outta here ya damn dawgs!" Jeb snarled. He kicked in their direction, a cloud of dirt wafting in the air. They looked at him with their heads cocked to the side, but didn't pay Jeb any mind and continued rooting around looking for scraps.

Jeb walked around the house, scanning the tree line looking for any sign of Pa. He walked along looking at the trees before coming to their well. He stepped near the well and looked inside, hoping not to find Pa floating in the dark water. Sweat dripped off his forehead. After several minutes staring in the well, Jeb figured Pa wasn't there and continued towards the back of the house.

About fifty yards from the house stood their large weathered barn. Pa told Jeb it used to be a bright red color, but the rain and sun worked it over like a prize-fighter and now it stood as a faded remnant of what it used to be. They didn't have many animals and most weren't in the barn anyway. They used it for storing tools and equipment. Pa sometimes liked to spend his time sharpening tools. Jeb decided to look inside.

He walked to the barn door. One of the coon-hounds ran to Jeb, his wagging tail creating a small cloud of dust behind him. Jeb kicked it. The dog yelped when Jeb's boot caught it in the ribs. "Git outta here ya damn dog!" Jeb yelled. The dog ran to the woods. Jeb stopped just short of the barn door listening for Pa and the familiar scrape of file on steel. No sound came from inside.

Jeb pulled the weathered door. It creaked as he opened it.

When he stepped inside, his eyes bulged and he wanted to scream, but the sound wouldn't leave his throat.

Standing before him were several small green creatures. Jeb thought they looked somewhat human, except they had one large red eye in the center of their foreheads and it blinked rapidly at him. "What the fu.." he said when one of the green creatures raised its hand, showing three thick fingers, silencing Jeb.

The creatures chattered amongst themselves, gesturing towards Jeb and at the back of the barn. Their clicking sounds sent shivers up Jeb's spine. His feet froze in place. Like his voice, his feet wouldn't respond to the direction of his brain.

One of the small green creatures rushed to Jeb's side. A sharp pain shot up his leg where the thing grabbed him. Instant electric agony pulsed through him dropping Jeb to the ground in wild convulsions. The little green creatures surrounded him. With a quick motion they lifted him off the ground, carrying him as if on a stretcher to the farthest wall of the barn where one of the things gestured earlier.

Jeb could still see, though his ability to move or talk was hindered by the creature's touch. They laid him in a pool of warm liquid. He tried turning his head but it didn't move. One creature leaned in and stared in Jeb's eyes. He wanted to scream, but the touch stifled it. Fear raced through him. *I don't wanna die! Pa, help me!* Jeb screamed in his head. The creatures lifted him so he was standing again. The moment they did, he wished they hadn't.

Pa's spent carcass lay on the dirt floor in front of him. The blood had been removed, revealing a heap of skin, bones, and muscle. His head was split in the middle with his brain partially removed. The chattering rose again, but then something changed. They sounded human.

"Great job Ervina! You did well," he heard a creature say. "You've passed your exam, you brought the human to us, and now you graduate with honors." A loud cry ascended from the creatures deafening Jeb. They clapped their small stubby-fingered hands. One creature stepped in front of Jeb, its sickly green skin stretched taut over its small frame. Its large eyes looked at Jeb, blinking slowly.

"Graduate! Graduate!" it said in clear English.

"Yes Ervina, you graduate. Now claim your reward."

The creature in front of Jeb stuck out its finger, piercing Jeb's side just below his ribs. Blood oozed out and the creature latched on to the wound with its small mouth. Jeb felt his blood draining from his body.

"Graduate!" they said again as his world went dark.

STORY TWELVE
DREAMWRAITH

A warm darkness permeated the bedroom. It promised to suffocate any living thing. The inky blackness shrouded the entire room in a hopeless gloom. The only visible objects were the sharp, crooked fangs of the dreamwraith looming over its prey.

Under a patchwork quilt stitched together by her grandmother's wrinkled, loving hands, Shannon lay in a deep sleep, unaware of the evil hovering just above her. Soft blonde curls encompassed her face in gentle caresses. Her body grew and shrank with each deep breath.

Above her, the dreamwraith grinned. His black cloak unnecessary in the late hours as the moon dared not shine this night. "I'm ready to feast," he said. His wispy voice carried across the dark room. He learned long ago that at this hour, his chances of being caught were slim. The chance existed, but that was only one of many things that excited him about being a dreamwraith.

"My lovely Shannon, how I've missed you. I've been waiting to feast upon your dreams once again. Their flavor so delicate and succulent. Feed me well yet again," the dreamwraith said. His white eyes darted up and down the bed looking at the gentle woman sleeping unaware of her visitor.

Shannon was young and still in college working on her degree in Medieval literature. A degree almost worthless in rural Ohio, but yet she stuck with her passion to the dismay of her parents.

Shifting her position on the bed, she lay on her stomach, one leg hanging out of the quilt. Saliva dripped from the dreamwraith's mouth as Shannon's movement made his heartbeat quicken.

With a long bony hand, the dreamwraith reached out and palmed her head. His vision turned from oppressive black to vibrant blues and deep verdant shades. A forest with a mighty river flowing to his right burst into view. The rushing water crashed on rocks which stuck out from the river like sentries.

The dreamwraith smiled again. He cherished the sweetness of Shannon's dream, could taste the overwhelming freedom and his urges pushed him over the edge. He stood there on a field of green dotted with yellows and reds and violets in his black cloak, a jarring reminder of his task to take away the dreams of humans.

He reached out to the ground and scraped at it with his gray-boned fingers shoving the delicacy in his mouth. He closed his eyes as he relished the sweet nectar of Shannon's dream. The honey-like consistency coated his mouth and throat. He choked on it, but that was why he came back. No other dreams he'd eaten tasted like hers.

His kind was forbidden any personal attachments. They were directed to go from one to another lest the humans discover them. Dreamwraiths had been caught over the years, but they always figured out a way to silence the person. They were forced to wait five years before returning to any human. That was enough time for the person to forget anything out of the ordinary happened.

But he couldn't stay away.

This was the dreamwraith's third visit to Shannon in the past year. Her dreams were a powerful drug, an addiction he couldn't get rid of even if he wanted to. Just the thought of them made his knees tremble and his mouth water. When the inferior dreams no longer satisfied him, he visited Shannon to feast on her exquisite, sumptuous gift.

He scraped more of her dream from the ground shoving it in his mouth. His mouth exploded in vibrant, exotic flavors. The unique taste of her dreams coursed through him. It fueled a lust deep within. He dropped to the ground and with both bony hands, shoveled the dream into his open maw, greedily gorging on the delectable dream.

Shannon stirred. The dreamwratih found itself in the dark bedroom again. "No," it hissed, "you must stay asleep my dear. You will not turn me away." His blank white eyes stared at her. He lifted his hand to her head again and stood in the green fields once more. At once he dropped to the ground and returned to his gorging, his entire being caught up in the orgiastic pleasure of her dream.

In no time he devoured almost the entire dream, his hunger still not sated. He stood a moment in the void of what was once her dream with only a small section of blue and green color left. Savoring the taste of his last bite, he let the flavor wash over him.

Shannon moved and he knew his time was shortening. Lunging at the spot of color still visible in the dream, he tore at it, shoving it in his mouth, filling himself with her essence. The moment he took the last bite of her dream, he found himself back in the dark bedroom.

It wasn't as dark as before. The tendrils of morning seeped in, breaking the doom of night. Slowly the dreamwraith backed away, his lust fulfilled. He crept towards the corner of the room as Shannon moved on the bed. The patchwork quilt tossed to one side while she moved her arms and rubbed her legs together. The dreamwraith grinned as he stared at Shannon. He knew what she tasted like and it was his secret. She raised from the bed and he winked out of the room, satisfied for now.

***

Shannon awoke feeling tired as though she hadn't slept in a long time. *Why am I still so tired?* she thought. For the rest of the day, Shannon couldn't drink enough coffee or energy drinks to keep her alert and awake. It reminded her of pulling an all-nighter yet she slept for over eight hours the night before. When she got home from school, she ate a quick dinner and went to bed. Her mind and body were completely exhausted. Never knowing why she spent the day with her eyes half open, Shannon drifted off to a peaceful slumber.

STORY THIRTEEN
MISSING THE OBVIOUS

Turning around to face the crowd, Angela's eyes went straight to her boyfriend Tony. But instead of catching her performance, Tony was kissing another girl.

"That bitch!" Angela said. She continued performing their routine, pom-poms shaking and skirts flying. It was half-time and the Blue Devils and Warriors were tied at 14. Angela's squad had a brief performance before going back to the sidelines for the second half. That's when she'd look for Tony and blow him a secret kiss.

But this time, his lips locked with Anne, that slutty new girl from Indiana.

Angela seethed. But as she watched Tony and Anne, she noticed something above their heads, something she'd never seen before. Images floated above them. A car above Tony and a gun above Anne.

Angela almost lost her place in the routine. Images appeared above the crowd, jumbled and confusing. They were everywhere. She felt dizzy and fell. She ran off the field embarrassed. And pissed.

A few minutes later Tony found her behind the bleachers.

"Hey, what's wrong babe?" he said. Through her tears, she could still make out the car above Tony. It looked like his dark blue Camaro. She wiped her face.

"Why were you kissing her?" Angela asked. Her face streaked with black mascara.

"I...I..." Tony said. He closed his mouth.

"Yeah, that's what I thought. Just leave," Angela said. She couldn't take her eyes off the car above Tony's head. It floated in a shimmering cloud.

"But Angela," Tony said.

"But what? Don't say any more Tony. Please leave me."

Tony turned to walk away.

"Tony," Angela called to him.

He turned, excitement showing on his face.

"Be careful, she might shoot you." She smiled as tears lined her cheek falling to the ground.

Tony looked at her, opened his mouth to reply, then left.

The next day as Angela half-heartedly ate her cereal, the newscaster on tv reported a young couple in her hometown were killed the night before. The girl by a gunshot to the head and the young man by car accident. Apparently they were being carjacked and when the gunman shot the girl, the guy sped away only to slam into a tree a quarter mile down the road. The news reporter didn't say who they were, but Angela knew.

She dropped her spoon and shook in her seat. Her eyes were wide with shock.

"The images," she said under her breath. Her mom overheard her.

"What dear? I hope they weren't friends of yours. Poor kids. I bet their parents are heartbroken."

Angela hadn't told her mom about Tony and the slut yet.

A vision appeared above her mom's head like she'd seen above Tony's. Floating above her was a butterfly drifting around a small bush. She didn't understand what it meant.

"Mom, I know who they were. It was Tony and this new girl Anne. They kissed last night and I saw something above their heads, like a cloud but with pictures. A gun loomed over Anne and a car over Tony." She sobbed.

Her mom caressed Angela's head. "Oh dear, I'm so sorry." She leaned in and gave Angela a tight hug, holding her close.

"But mom, I see images. I see things. You have one right now. It's a butterfly fluttering around a bush. It's right there," Angela said pointing to the space above her mom's head. Her mom rocked her.

"There there dear. It's alright. It'll be fine. You're in shock."

Several weeks after the tragedy, Angela told close friends at school about her visions. More often than not, they laughed at her or gave her a gentle pat knowing she'd lost her boyfriend in a terrible way. "No, I don't want pity. You've got to believe me! I see things," she protested. No one listened.

Later that year after winter had let up and spring thawed the ground, Angela's mother went hiking in the woods with a friend. She'd gone several times before and thought nothing of it. Butterflies still fluttered above her mom's head and Angela tried conveying to her the importance of it.

"Mom, please be careful. If you see a butterfly, run. Or something. I don't know. Be careful," Angela said to her mom as she left. Her mom smiled.

"Dear, if I see a butterfly, I'll run the other way. Now rest, this year has been hard on you. I'll be back in a few hours."

She never came home.

She was found dead by a bush with butterflies gently floating about. It was then that Angela decided she'd had enough. No one listened to her when she told them what she saw. They only mocked her or thought she was under overwhelming stress.

Angela went to live with her grandma after her mother's death. Her dad left them long ago.

One day as she sat in a chair on the back patio, she watched as a butterfly with orange and black wings flitted by, dancing in the air. Anger swelled inside her. She jumped up, grabbed the car keys, and sped off, driving nowhere in particular.

As she drove on a lonely two lane highway, she heard sirens. Behind her a blue Camaro, similar to Tony's, was speeding towards her with police cars chasing after it. She pulled off the road.

A gunshot cracked the air and the Camaro swerved violently, slamming into her car killing her. When the paramedics arrived, they marveled at the butterflies dancing around the wreck, their orange and black wings contrasting with the grisly scene.

STORY FOURTEEN
THE GEM AND THE HIDE

Gerald approached the cave, his heart beating a thunderous tone in his chest. Lady Ygraine needed the gems from deep within the cave at the wizard Shonar's request in order for her kingdom to be free of the dark Lord Mormet. As her champion, Gerald's sworn duty was to her. He was Lady Ygraine's only hope. He'd not fail her now.

Gerald wiped his brow and stepped inside holding a lit torch.

He wound his way through endless tunnels, following the map given to him by Lady Ygraine. He found sparkling green and blue gems encrusted in the walls of an inner chamber. Reaching out to pry an extraordinary bright green gem from the cave's wall, the room started spinning. The floor disappeared from under him and he fell for a long time only to land unharmed on soft ground.

Gerald found himself surrounded by thousands of blinking lights, twinkling their song. He shielded his eyes from the visual onslaught.

"What pray tell are ye that flashes this infernal device! Yield. I yield!" he shouted to the lights. A strange series of clicking sounds enveloped him. With a flash, everything turned bright white then stopped.

He felt solid ground underneath and stood. He couldn't see a thing.

"I must leave this cursed cave before more vile or hideous acts befall me," he said. He extended his hands in the blinding whiteness but found no walls nor gems which to hold. He searched for anything to get him out.

Nothing.

He walked straight ahead, arms outstretched, searching for a wall or any surface with which to guide himself.

He stepped on a soft, squishy substance and stopped. Bending down, he nudged the viscous material. It was warm to the touch and gave just the slightest. Surprised, Gerald stood up and continued his cautious walk forward.

Ferocious hot air fueled by enormous flames whooshed past him, singeing his beard.

"By the gods, what hell am I in?" he said.

"Lost knight, you are in my home. My sanctuary. You are an intruder."

"Who's there?" Gerald called to the voice. Thin tendrils of smoke wafted from his mustache and eyebrows. He patted them hoping to extinguish whatever small flame caused it.

"I do not answer to mortals of the fifth realm. You are in my home, you answer to me."

The voice was harsh, raspy, and male.

"I am Gerald of the Moors, champion of Lady Ygraine, the keeper of the Valley. I kneel to no one!" he replied.

The voice cackled. "Then why do you yield with such haste champion?"

Gerald bent his head low.

"You are nothing knight. You are in my home Gerald. Why do you bother me in the seventh realm? You don't belong here."

"I'm on a quest to retrieve jewels from this cave. My Lady needs them to save her kingdom. Will you help me?"

Another loud, long laugh from the voice. "I told you Gerald, you don't belong here. You are far from home. Because of your intrusion, you are my champion now. You do *my* bidding."

Gerald's heart sank. His beloved Ygraine, the only Lady he'd ever truly loved was lost to him. This formless voice now commanded him.

The voice spoke out again. "If you do my bidding, I might be kind enough to send you back to your dimension. Fail me, and your soul belongs to me. Forever!"

Gerald wrung his hands, thinking over the proposal.

"Spirit, my life is yours to command. I give to you my service so I may return to my Lady Ygraine," Gerald replied. A soft cackle answered him.

"You will bring me the hide of a boar. It needs be white in color and red of eye. Bring it back within a fortnight and your realm I will send you. Now go!"

Before Gerald could reply, the scene shifted again like a veil removed from his eyes. He stood in an old forest full of large trees unfamiliar to him. He spun around searching for the cave. Light twinkled from a knot in the nearest tree. He stepped towards it.

"I said go! Return when you've acquired the hide or your soul is mine," the voice said from the twinkling knot. Gerald marked the tree with his sword and took off in search of his quarry.

After seven days of fruitless searching, Gerald lost hope. He saw no boar. Late the afternoon of the seventh day as he sat under a tall tree enjoying the comforts of the shade, he spotted it.

Across from him about fifty paces away was the beast. It was larger than any man and whiter than snow. It snorted and rooted in the dirt, covering its snout with brown and black.

Gerald's eyes lit up. Hope burst through his veins. He crouched low and made his way towards the boar as silent as possible. When he was within ten paces, he drew his sword and lunged. The beast jerked its head up at the sound but it was too late. Gerald thrust his blade deep in its heart, killing it. He skinned it and hurried back to the knot in the tree.

A brilliant light shone from the knot and Gerald again found himself inside the white nothingness though this time holding the hide of the slain boar.

"I have your treasure, now grant my boon as promised," Gerald said to the nothingness. Silence. "Spirit, listen! I have your bounty, now grant me my release!" To his right, Gerald heard the soft familiar cackle.

"So, you've slain the beast, eh? My what a diligent knight you are. A promise is a promise."

The hide disappeared and Gerald fell once again into a void until he landed on hard ground. He pushed himself off the ground and recognized the cave. Gerald seized green and blue gems and ran out as fast as he could.

Upon his return to the castle, Lady Ygraine marveled at his success.

"Your absence so long I feared Lord Mormet would gain the kingdom. You truly are my hero!" She kissed him, causing his cheeks to blush.

"You have done a wonderful thing here Gerald. Your actions saved the kingdom. Lord Mormet did not attain the sacred hide from the seventh realm," Lady Ygraine said.

Gerald's face turned white. He spun around to face the wizard Shonar.

"What sorcery are you about Shonar? Tell me!" Gerald shouted. Shonar shrugged.

"None good knight. Because of your deeds, Lord Mormet failed to secure the hide. These gems would be powerless if he had. He'd soon rule this kingdom and we'd be helpless to stop him," Shonar replied.

"But how do you know of the hide?" Gerald asked.

Shonar waved a hand in the air. "Wizards divine much Gerald. It's what we do."

Shonar walked away and Gerald swore he heard an unmistakable soft cackle as the wizard strode along the walkway, a faint glow surrounding his body.

STORY FIFTEEN
BROTHERS NO MORE

"Time. Time to eat. Eat now. Right? I eat now. Hungry I am. I eat. Go, now!"

"No, we're just fine. You ate a few hours ago. There's no need to gorge ourselves. Hell, look at our gut! It's huge. We really need to go on a diet. It's not good for our health."

"No! Eat! Gregor hungry! Need food. Belly. Hungry. Eat!"

"Now listen Gregor, we'll have dinner in a couple hours. We need nothing right now. Maybe a glass of water? I've read if you feel hungry, then it might only be your body telling you it's in need of water and if you drink water your hunger will go…"

"No water, food! Hungry! Eat now. Gregor eat now!"

"I told you we're not eating right now. We'll get water. I've got a pitcher of cold water here in the fridge. We'll start there. If you're still hungry after that, then we'll get a snack. But something healthy, not the normal meat and fat packed bits of nastiness you gorge on."

Gregor grumbled but Eric ignored him and poured a tall glass of cold water. He handed it to Gregor who downed it in one large gulp.

"Now, isn't that better? Let that sit for a moment and we'll see if we still need that snack." Eric poured another glass and sipped, letting the cool water quench his parched tongue. He enjoyed a tall glass of cold water in the middle of a hot day and with the temperature reaching close to 95, it felt especially refreshing. He walked outside and sat on a metal grate chair on the deck looking over their back yard.

Birds flittered amongst the trees, squirrels chattered back and forth to each other. A cardinal hopped around the grass near their garden. He loved to sit out on the deck, under the umbrella, and just watch nature unfold in front of him.

Gregor didn't have the same appreciation. He'd rather grab a rock and heave it at anything that was unfortunate enough to scurry by. Once he struck a squirrel in the head. The thing flipped in the air landing on its side convulsing. Gregor watched it with an evil fascination. Eric had to put the poor creature out of its misery, the suffering too demented for him.

"Eat! Food. Eat now?" Gregor asked. His tough voice held a touch of whininess. Eric closed his eyes and pinched the bridge of his nose. He breathed long deep breaths.

"Gregor," he said in a flat tone, "It. Is. Not. Time. To. Eat." He punctuated each word as though speaking to a child. He kept his voice on the edge of calm.

"But," Gregor began. "But hungry. Please. Eat."

Eric slammed his fist on the metal table making his glass tumble over and crash to the deck. It broke when it slammed on the wood, scattering shards of glass and water. "Gregor, there will be no snack! No more!" Eric said.

Gregor wouldn't listen. "Need food. Hungry. Eric. Food. Now. Gregor need food! Gregor need eat!"

Jumping up from his seat, Eric knocked the chair backwards. "I told you Gregor, no food now. You've had enough." The veins in Eric's forehead bulged, pulsing with each angry breath.

"No! Gregor eat. Food," Gregor replied.

Eric's face twisted in disbelief. Gregor had never disobeyed Eric. He hesitated, wondering what to do. He couldn't let him get away with his blatant disregard for Eric's authority. Eric had always been the one in charge and Gregor the one to fall in line. For whatever reason, Gregor argued with Eric, something he'd never done before.

Eric understood what he had to do. He dreaded this moment since they were young. He prepared but still loathed it. The back door led straight to the kitchen and Eric walked towards the house.

"Yes! Gregor eat. Food," Gregor said as they stepped through the door into the kitchen.

Eric's arms shook the tiniest bit. Because it had to be done didn't make it any easier.

"What do you want Gregor? What kind of snack must you have to shut your infernal mouth?" Eric said.

Gregor grew excited at the prospect of getting a snack. "Meat. Gregor eat. Meat. Please Eric?" he replied.

Gregor had an insatiable appetite for flesh. He enjoyed the large, muscular pieces they'd get from meatheads that frequented the gym. They were careful not to be too greedy and Eric learned how to preserve the meat making it last a long time. No one ever suspected Gregor of the crimes either. Eric didn't perform the actual kidnapping and killing, so he was in the clear. Though once they got home with their meat, Eric had to butcher it. It always made his stomach lurch and he'd vomit every time they carved an arm or leg off, but he did the work.

This time however, he didn't intend on letting Gregor have his snack. Gregor's insatiable appetite had increased their girth. Eric bought a whole new set of pants four months ago and they were already too tight. Gregor was out of control and it was time to do something.

Eric opened a drawer as if to get the butcher knife, but instead grabbed the meat thermometer. Gregor didn't notice.

"Gregor, it's time. I'm so sorry," Eric said, the thermometer's metallic point raised to his right eye. He knew where Gregor lived. He'd always known where he lived. Pain scared him but he had to do what needed to be done.

He always had.

With both hands gripping the round rubbery dial of the

thermometer, Eric drew it towards his eye.

"Gregor eat. Hungry. Meat. Meat. Food!" Gregor said. He was oblivious to Eric.

With a determined thrust, Eric drove the thermometer into his right eye, his vision going black. Searing pain shot through his head. He heard a wet pop as he impaled his eye. Gregor screamed an awful sound.

"No!" Gregor yelled. "Why? Only. Hungry. Eric!" he yelled. Eric pushed the thermometer in further causing an intense stinging sensation. He felt pressure from the thermometer inside his head, the point thrusting itself through his eye to the small place where Gregor lived.

"I...I...I had to Gregor. Please forgive me," Eric said, his voice barely above a whisper. Gregor screamed in agony within Eric's brain. He howled and wailed as his life faded. Then all went silent. Gregor was gone. Only his echo remained.

Eric pulled on the thermometer, each move tugging at his eye until it came out of the socket still attached to the thermometer. He cried out from the pain.

Then his lips twisted into a smile as he laid the thermometer on the table with his once blue eye impaled on it.

He no longer had to suffer through Gregor's infantile rants, and he no longer needed the meatheads from the gym. From now on, he would live free.

STORY SIXTEEN
THE LONG SLEEP

Ivor awoke coughing. Deep in his lungs sat a heavy choking gel. Waking should have been smooth and painless.

The last thing he remembered were the agronomical implications of system failure. It was taught to all colonists. Or deserters. Or visionaries. They went by many names depending on your point of view.

The long trek across the cosmos required cryo-sleep as the safest solution for depositing them at their destination alive. During the "long sleep" their brains were hard-wired to the on-board AI which acted as doctor, parent, and teacher to the colonists. Ivor was in the middle of a lecture with at least two-hundred other colonists when jolted from his class coughing and gasping for air.

With his eyes opened in the dark room, small lights appeared brilliant. Reds and blues and greens so bright he tried to shield his eyes though the lights themselves only gave off tiny pinpricks which penetrated the clear protective canopy covering him. The close fitting canopy prevented him from covering his face with his hands.

Sudden claustrophobia overwhelmed him. It felt like the first time he lay in the cryo-chamber. At the time the AI tried reassuring him but when its soothing failed, it turned to more aggressive measures and sedated him with a cocktail of drugs Ivor's physically fit body couldn't overcome. Before long he passed out in the chamber sleeping until now. He struggled against the canopy and with great effort breached the seal flinging it open crashing it to the floor.

Ivor rose to a seated position stabilizing himself on the edges of the bed. His arms shook. His entire body shivered. In deep space, the ship maintained just enough heat to keep instruments from freezing. Humans in cryo-sleep required minimal warmth.

Ivor listened as every tiny noise seemed louder than ever.

The colonists were taught that coming out of cryo-sleep too fast made for an excruciating snap back to reality. A person's senses were super-hyper and the tiniest light, sound, and smell pushed their brains to its limits as it tried to adjust to its environment once again. Ivor understood that now.

As his brain adjusted, he realized there were no sounds of people. The AI didn't scream at him. In fact it was silent. And dark except for the few tiny indicator lights.

Ivor climbed out of the bed and fell to the floor, his legs not adjusted to standing yet. His naked body flailed on the cold metal floor sending extreme cold sensations through him. Looking around in the dark, he spotted his personal locker. Inside should be clothes issued to him like every colonist before the journey.

He dragged his limp body across the floor leaving a trail of cold gel. His teeth chattered. Wisps of mist fluttered in his face with each exhaled breath. With a great effort, Ivor reached his locker. He keyed in his code and the locker whooshed open. A light blinked on inside the locker revealing three sets of standard issue navy blue coveralls with undergarments and one pair of boots. He yanked down an undershirt and dried himself.

Grabbing the locker door, he pulled himself up to a sitting position and struggled to get dressed. In time he stopped shivering and regained the ability to walk.

Ivor found a lantern in his locker and went in search of others.

Outside his room in the dark hallway alarmed him. If he were at their destination, there should be others. The AI should've been barking orders or chatting with the other colonists. Instead silence echoed the darkness.

Something was wrong.

Ivor clung to the metallic walls as he made his way down the empty black corridor. Not a single soul stirred. The constant hum of the ship's atmospheric system the only sound. *Well*, he thought, *at least I have that going for me.* It was little consolation, but gave him a shred of hope.

After searching several levels of the ship and finding no one, Ivor wondered if something catastrophic happened to the ship. A hull breach? An alien attack? A governmental policy?

Their departure from Earth had its critics. And it was not beyond reason to believe the United National Congress had somehow sabotaged the ship. A hard-line group of Congress members vehemently opposed the venture complaining it cost too much for a possible colonization and that money should be spent on the immediate needs of the burgeoning humanitarian crisis.

That's what they kept calling it. A "possible" colonization as though all the data collected, all the research, and all the findings didn't point to a habitable planet for the continued existence of humanity. When the bureaucrats finally had their way and cut off funding, a private organization stepped in to continue the project. No funding came through the United National Congress.

After a careful selection of colonists, the project pushed forward. Seven hundred colonists chosen based on desired genetics committed to a one-way trip to Kepler 186f.

It was a daring plan, but since the discovery of a wormhole that bridged the Milky Way with Kepler 186f, it grew feasible. And with the total global conflict raging to the point where spotting the sun through artificial clouds made of toxic dust and other debris was cause for celebration, it was time to go.

Ivor stood in a dark hallway two levels up from where he started, thinking the mission was doomed and isolation set in. Where were the others? Not long ago he sat in a virtual class with many of them studying agronomical problems, yet he couldn't find a single person.

The hallways lit up, artificial light flooding every corridor chasing away the darkness. An alarm screamed to life. Ivor dropped his lantern and covered his ears against the wailing. Red lights flashed along the corridor.

"Colonist 2521433, you are in breach of contract. You must return to your chambers immediately for reintroduction to cryo-sleep," the ship's AI boomed at Ivor. The voice came from everywhere. "Colonist 2521433, return to your chambers," it said again. A door whooshed open at the far end of the hall and three small bots scurried out towards Ivor.

He'd seen these before in one of his lessons while in cryo-sleep. The AI was deliberate in the lesson telling the colonists these bots were small yet the most lethal elements of the ship. Originally planned as safeguards to hostile alien encounters they were also programmed with a secondary function as an internal police force. More than once the AI demonstrated their lethality in class. Ivor ran down the hall, stumbling a few times as if drunk, determined to escape them.

At the end of the hall, it branched into two separate corridors. Running down the left one, Ivor was lost.

"Colonist 2521433 you are ordered to stop! Lethal force is authorized by command 77456-ST1. There is no escape. Running will only lead to undesired dire consequences," the omnipresent AI shouted at Ivor. Winded from the short run, Ivor stumbled the last few steps in the corridor. The AI turned off the lights attempting to trap Ivor. It worked.

Ivor slammed headfirst into a solid metal wall. Warm liquid trickled down his face and he crashed to the floor. The force of the impact winded him. Gasping for air, struggling on the cold metallic floor, Ivor couldn't get up before the three small bots were on him. A tiny point of light emanated from one of them, then all of them.

Catching his breath at last, Ivor yelled, "No!" while the lights grew brighter.

"I warned you Colonist 2521433. They are authorized by command 77456-ST1 to use lethal force. However…"

Ivor's heart jumped in his chest. "However?" he said.

"I have instructed them otherwise. You will follow instructions Colonist 2521433. It was unwise of you to run. Your body is not ready for such feats. No matter, it will be soon enough."

Ivor screamed as one of the small bots punctured his skin with what felt like a needle. Hot stinging pain ran up his arm towards his chest and spread out like thousands of tiny nanobots coursing through his body. Ivor's screams echoed in the dark empty corridor. He writhed on the floor tearing at his chest as if to remove the pain. It didn't help. Soon he passed out and collapsed into black nothingness.

The bots picked him off the floor and carted him back to his cryo-chamber. With little effort, they placed him in his chamber, hooked up the respirator, and started the cryo-process again. The lid closed to the sound of escaping air as it sealed tight.

"He's back in stasis my lord," the AI said.

"Good. He almost ruined the mission. Never let that happen again, do you hear me? I paid good money to have control over you and this is how you repay me? I expected better of you. Don't screw it up. We have a mission to complete," the only awake human said to the AI. She stood in Ivor's room looking in his chamber at his face so peaceful.

"He might be one of the lucky ones. That kind of determination goes far. We might have a use for him yet," she said.

"Yes my lord. I will keep an eye on him and will not let the others harm him unless you wish it."

"Myrthyd, please play some of that old blues music I'm fond of. And get started with the virus. Seems like now would be the perfect time to sterilize my enemies. Can't have too many rivals going after my prizes. I will remake humanity in my image. One day, they will call out to me. They will remember me as their creator. They will never forget Anastasia."

"As you wish my lord. Commencing virus replication in all females on board. By the time we reach Kepler 186f, your place will be permanent among the colony. Might I suggest we rename the planet in your honor as well?"

Anastasia smiled and broke out in laughter. "Myrthyd, you are worth the money! Yes, yes we will. Program that in the colonists. And keep us on course for planet Anastasia!"

ABOUT THE AUTHOR

Originally a Cleveland, OH native, Jason currently lives in Southern Illinois with his wife, son, and small zoo of cats and dogs. As a novelist, video game story writer, and author of more than two dozen flash fiction works, he's been busy sharing odd stories with his readers.

He can be found regularly writing on his blog almostaverageblog.wordpress.com where he offers essays and original fiction.

Jason spends his leisure time as a loyal Cleveland Browns and Cleveland Cavaliers fan and moonlights as a promotional products sales rep.

Made in the USA
Charleston, SC
12 April 2016